YASMIN

The Scientist

written by
SAADIA FARUQI

illustrated by
HATEM ALY

PICTURE WINDOW BOOKS
a capstone imprint

To Mariam for inspiring me, and Mubashir
for helping me find the right words—S.F.

To my sister, Eman, and her amazing girls,
Jana and Kenzi—H.A.

Yasmin is published by Picture Window Books, an imprint of Capstone.
1710 Roe Crest Drive
North Mankato, Minnesota 56003
www.capstonepub.com

Text copyright © 2021 by Saadia Faruqi.
Illustrations copyright © 2021 by Capstone.

Library of Congress Cataloging-in-Publication Data is available on the
Library of Congress website.
Names: Faruqi, Saadia, author. | Aly, Hatem, illustrator. Title: Yasmin
the scientist / written by Saadia Faruqi ; illustrated by Hatem Aly.
Description: North Mankato, Minnesota : Capstone Press, [2021]
| Series: Yasmin | Audience: Ages 5-7. | Audience: Grades K-1. |
Summary: Everyone seems to have an idea for the science fair except
for Yasmin, but after some failed experiments, Yasmin's snack break
with Nani inspires an idea. Identifiers: LCCN 2020038988 (print) |
LCCN 2020038989 (ebook) | ISBN 9781515882602 (hardcover) | ISBN
9781515883739 (paperback) | ISBN 9781515892519 (pdf) | ISBN
9781515893271 (kindle edition) Subjects: CYAC: Science fairs—Fiction.
| Schools—Fiction. | Pakistani Americans—Fiction. | Muslims—United
States—Fiction. Classification: LCC PZ7.1.F373 Yit 2021 (print) | LCC
PZ7.1.F373 (ebook) | DDC [E]—dc23 LC record available at https://
lccn.loc.gov/2020038988 LC ebook record available at https://lccn.loc.
gov/2020038989

Editorial Credits:
Editor: Kristen Mohn; Designer: Kay Fraser; Production Specialist:
Tori Abraham

Design Elements:
Shutterstock: LiukasArt

TABLE OF CONTENTS

Chapter 1
SCIENCE NEWS.................................5

Chapter 2
A VOLCANO MESS.........................10

Chapter 3
A DELICIOUS EXPERIMENT.................20

CHAPTER 1

Science News

Ms. Alex had finished the science lesson. "Remember, the science fair is next week," she said.

The science fair? Yasmin had forgotten all about it!

"What do we make?" Yasmin whispered to Ali.

"Anything we like!" Ali said.
That wasn't very helpful!
Coming up with an idea was
hard. What if Yasmin couldn't
think of one?

Ms. Alex heard them. "Don't worry, Yasmin. You'll think of something," she said. "After all, science is all around us. Outside. In our classroom. Even in our kitchens!"

"Like when Mama cooks dinner?" Yasmin asked.

Ms. Alex smiled. "Yes. Cooking is also science!"

After school, Yasmin asked Mama, "What should I make for the science fair?"

Mama was busy in the kitchen. "Ideas are everywhere, jaan!"

Not helpful!

Soon Baba came home from work.

"Baba, I need an idea for the science fair," Yasmin said.

"I made an erupting volcano

when I was your age," he said.

"It was fantastic!"

CHAPTER 2

A Volcano Mess

Baba showed Yasmin videos of kids making volcanoes. Some volcanoes were big and tall. Others were short and colorful. All of them made a mess.

"Science is messy," Yasmin complained.

Baba nodded. "Sometimes *learning* is messy, jaan!" he said. "Don't worry."

On Saturday, Baba and Yasmin gathered supplies. Clay from Yasmin's room. Vinegar and baking soda from the kitchen.

"Would you like me to help you?" Baba asked Yasmin.

"I want to try this by myself," Yasmin said.

Baba patted her shoulder.

"I'll be in the living room if you need me," he said.

Yasmin got to work. She read the instructions they had printed. She shaped a volcano out of clay.

Her first try didn't look

anything like a volcano.

On her second try, there were

no bubbles.

On her third try, she spilled

vinegar everywhere. Her volcano

was a mess!

Yasmin stomped her foot.

What was she going to do?

Nani entered the kitchen.

"How about a lemonade

break?" she asked.

Yasmin nodded. All this

science had made her thirsty!

Nani squeezed the lemons.

Then she got out the sugar cubes

she used for her tea.

Yasmin loved sugar cubes!

She popped one into her mouth.

She rolled two more cubes like

dice on the table. They landed in

some spilled baking soda.

Nani poured Yasmin some

lemonade. Yasmin put the two

sugar cubes into her glass.

Fizz! The lemonade popped
and bubbled. Yasmin gasped.
"My lemonade is erupting!"

CHAPTER 3

A Delicious Experiment

It was the day of the science fair. Yasmin got to school early.

"What will you be presenting, Yasmin?" Ms. Alex asked.

Yasmin held up a big bottle.

"Everyone gets a cup of lemonade!" she said proudly.

Ali looked confused. "That's

not a science project!"

"You'll see," Yasmin replied.

The students began to set up their projects. Everyone was excited to present them. Emma had grown beans in a jar. Ali was floating eggs in water.

Ms. Alex and Principal Nguyen took notes on each one.

Soon it was Yasmin's turn. First she lined up the paper cups. Then she poured the lemonade. Next she dropped in the sugar cubes. Finally, Yasmin stirred a little baking soda into each cup.

Pop! Bubble! Fizz! Everyone clapped.

"Amazing!" Ms. Alex said.

"Clever!" Principal Nguyen said.

"It's an erupting volcano—without the mess!" Yasmin said with a grin. "And delicious!"

Think About It, Talk About It

* If you could be in a science fair, what project would you present?

* Think of a time with schoolwork, an art project, or a game when you needed to try a couple different ideas before you found one that worked. What made you keep trying?

* Sometimes parents or grandparents are too busy to help. Sometimes you don't want their help! Think of a time that you wanted to do something on your own. Now think of a time when you asked for help. What was different about each time?

Learn Urdu with Yasmin!

Yasmin's family speaks both English and Urdu. Urdu is a language from Pakistan. Maybe you already know some Urdu words!

baba (BAH-bah)—father

hijab (HEE-jahb)—scarf covering the hair

jaan (jahn)—life; a sweet nickname for a loved one

kameez (kuh-MEEZ)—long tunic or shirt

lassi (LAH-see)—a yogurt drink

naan (nahn)—flatbread baked in the oven

nana (NAH-nah)—grandfather on mother's side

nani (NAH-nee)—grandmother on mother's side

salaam (sah-LAHM)—hello

shukriya (shuh-KREE-yuh)—thank you

Pakistan Fun Facts

Yasmin and her family are proud of their Pakistani culture. Yasmin loves to share facts about Pakistan!

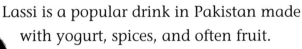

Pakistan is on the continent of Asia, with India on one side and Afghanistan on the other.

The word Pakistan means "land of the pure" in Urdu and Persian.

Many languages are spoken in Pakistan, including Urdu, English, Saraiki, Punjabi, Pashto, Sindhi, and Balochi.

Naan is a flatbread often served with meals in Pakistan.

Lassi is a popular drink in Pakistan made with yogurt, spices, and often fruit.

Make a Fizzy Lemonade

SUPPLIES:

- 2 glasses of cold water
- ½ cup lemon juice (fresh-squeezed or bottled)
- ½ cup finely granulated sugar
- a few sugar cubes
- 2 tablespoons baking soda

STEPS:

1. Mix together the water, lemon juice, and granulated sugar in a pitcher. Make sure the sugar is completely stirred in.

2. Put the baking soda on a small dish. Roll the sugar cubes in it.

3. Pour some of your lemonade into a glass.

4. Drop a sugar cube or two into the glass. Watch the fizz!

5. Drink the lemonade—it's perfectly safe!

About the Author

Saadia Faruqi is a Pakistani American writer, interfaith activist, and cultural sensitivity trainer featured in *O Magazine*. She is author of two middle grade novels, *A Place at the Table* and *A Thousand Questions*. She is also editor-in-chief of *Blue Minaret*, an online magazine of poetry, short stories, and art. Besides writing books, she also loves reading, binge-watching her favorite shows, and taking naps. She lives in Houston, Texas, with her husband and children.

About the Illustrator

Hatem Aly is an Egyptian-born illustrator whose work has been published all over the world. He currently lives in beautiful New Brunswick, Canada, with his wife, son, and more pets than people. When he is not dipping cookies in a cup of tea or staring at blank pieces of paper, he is usually drawing, reading, or daydreaming. You can see his art in books that earned multiple starred reviews and positions on the *NYT* Best-Sellers list, such as *The Proudest Blue* (with Ibtihaj Muhammad & S.K. Ali) and *The Inquisitor's Tale* (with Adam Gidwitz), a Newbery Honor winner.

Join Yasmin on all her adventures!